DATE DUE

How Jasper, a monkey from Africa, becomes
the toast of the theatre. The illustrations add
fascination to a moving story of a small,
subtle animal, seen with imagination.

B 2-749

MR. BUMPS AND HIS MONKEY

MR. BUMPS AND HIS MONKEY

by

WALTER DE LA MARE

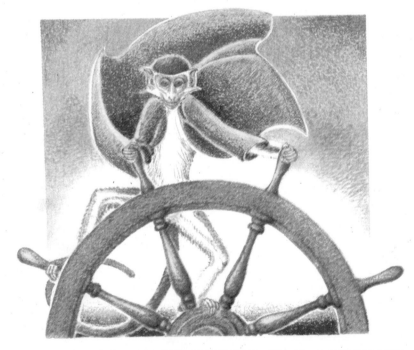

Illustrated by DOROTHY P. LATHROP

HOLT, RINEHART AND WINSTON
New York   Chicago   San Francisco

91798-0512

Printed in the United States of America

INTRODUCTION

Sometimes it seems as if there are only two kinds of people in the world, those who like animals, and those who don't. The first willingly share this earth with all its other creatures and, as they walk through it, instinctively peer up among the leaves or down between the grass for glimpses of wings or fur. Their ears are tuned to the singing of birds and their hands hang within reach of a dog's friendly muzzle. But the second feel that they are the earth's only lawful tenants and would infinitely prefer to walk through a world as neat and silent and empty as a treeless lawn. They will chatter even through a thrush's song.

Open any volume of Walter de la Mare's at random and one knows at once that he is keenly aware of all living things and that for him human experience is enriched by any contact however slight with bird or beast or even with gaping, goggling fish. Such an author one can imagine only in a country garden visited by nightingales, cuckoos, and small brown bunnies and, on a moonlit night, perhaps an old witch hare or two. But should he be condemned to live in the city—and it would "condemned" I am sure—sparrows seen through his poems would be as enchanting as skylarks, and as for the cats which prowl on backyard fences—well, we already have the matchless story of sinister, jet-black Sam who kept such unholy company.

Frequently his sympathy for creatures in a world dominated by man overflows into ironic or indignant verse. Who will forget "I can't abear a Butcher," or the fish who talked in the frying pan, or once read, this brief indictment:

> Hi! handsome hunting man,
> Fire your little gun.
> Bang! Now the animal
> Is dead and dumb and done.
> Nevermore to peep again, creep again, leap again,
> Eat or sleep or drink again, Oh, what fun! *

Only one with such sympathy could have written the story of Jasper, a little monkey captive in the alien world of man. For prisoner his body was in spite of the kindness of his two friends, Mr. Bumps and Mr. Smith, although no soul was ever more free within stone walls or iron bars than his.

Of all the creatures who throng Walter de la Mare's books, one feels that monkeys have a special place in his affections, for never has he created two personalities more wistful and endearing than Mr. Bumps' Jasper and Nod, the littlest and youngest of the three Mulla-Mulgars.

No one, I hope, will be misled by the jacket of this book into thinking this merely an animal story, and so miss a rare bit of imaginative writing. For Jasper, the author says, "was as different from other monkeys as chalk from cheese." Certainly the monkey who has been living with me now for some months and helping me with these illustrations has none of Jasper's cleverness in learning to speak the human tongue nor in adopting our customs, and would be quite incapable of walking the boards of a London stage with Jasper's

* From "Hi," in *Poems for Children*, by Walter de la Mare. Used by permission of the publisher, Henry Holt and Company, Inc.

iv

poise and regal bearing. This one is, I am afraid, as the Chief of the Mlango-Nlangoes would say, a "skittle-skattle monkey," and lately the word "monkeyshines" has assumed a new and often exasperating significance!

Walter de la Mare mentions a tiny monkey remembered from his infancy who considered crickets a delicacy. But this small one could hardly have furnished him with all his knowledge of that race, for know monkeys he does, as I see clearly now that I live so intimately with one. For Jasper is every inch a monkey in spite of what one is temped to call his almost human dignity. But how rare dignity is in humans! How seldom in the wall of staring faces at the zoo does it match that of the stared at—of the lion, the deer, the wolf, of almost any animal one can name. Often after hours of mischief and perversity and of conscious clowning, my "skittle-skattle" monkey will suddenly gaze at me with the same aloof pride and the same dwelling eyes which Mr. Moss found so hard to face. And how, for all his short stature, Jasper towers in spirit above the humans in the story, not only above those who exploit him, but above kind Mr. and Mrs. Smith and even his first friend, Mr. Bumps, who took him back at last to his own longed-for, native Africa.

I wonder if this perfect story, this humorous and poignant tale of a little super monkey is not as well a clearsighted glimpse of the spirit of any creature as it tries without bitterness to adapt itself to our wishes and our strange, incomprehensible ways.

Dorothy P. Lathrop

v

*T*HERE was once a sailor of the name of John Bumps. He had bright blue eyes and wore gold rings in his ears. Although, when this story begins, Mr. Bumps was still quite young, he had three children—Topsy, Emmanuel, and Kate—who lived with their mother in a nice little house with square windows in Portsmouth, and he had often been round the world. He had sailed into most of its ports in all kinds of weather; and there was scarcely an island of great beauty or marvel that he couldn't tick off on his tarry fingers.

Now one day, a little the right side of the rainy season, he came again to the west coast of Africa. His ship, *The Old Lion*—and he was her second mate—had

1

been sailing south down that great coast, past the Canaries and the Green Islands, past the Ivory and the Gold and the Slave Coasts to Banana and the noble Congo; and not long after that Mr. Bumps went ashore. He was paddled up the river Quanza, dark and green, past Dondo, to visit an old friend. And there in a village of the black men, for two green-and-red bead necklaces and a jackknife, he bought a monkey.

Mr. Bumps had now and then bought other monkeys, and he knew this was a high price for one in that part of the country. But his friend, the chief of the Mlango-Nlango tribe, who was exceedingly fat, and wore two blankets besides his beads and ivories, assured Mr. Bumps this was no ordinary monkey.

The chief's round, black face, with its two rows of flashing teeth, broke into an immense smile as he told Mr. Bumps this. "Ee no skittle-skattle monk-ee, no," he said, for he had often traded with the English. "Ee——," but instead of finishing the sentence, he shut his eyes and put one black hand on the top of his head, though what exactly he meant, Mr. Bumps could not tell. At first glimpse of the monkey, however, Mr. Bumps had known at once that whatever pleasant things the chief might say of it they would be true. Besides, the

2

chief was an old friend of his, and wouldn't tell him lies.

On the other hand, since the hairy little fellow stood an inch or so under the common stature of monkeys of its kind, it was of no great size, and there was nothing else remarkable that showed—not then. As Mr. Bumps held it on his arm, in its long-skirted crimson coat, which one of the chief's wives had made out of the royal cloth, it sat far less heavy indeed than would his younger daughter, Kate. And she herself was very small for her age.

But it had a neat, pretty head, wonderfully slender hands, and long thumbs, and as it turned its solemn hazel eyes on Mr. Bumps, he suddenly felt acutely homesick. He had been more than once more than half round the world without feeling *that*. "It's *no good* longing," he would say, "when you've got to wait."

And then something which Mr. Bumps had not expected at all happened. It was this. His eyes, as has been said already, were of a particularly bright blue; and as the blue of his blue eyes met the gazing hazel of the monkey's, the creature stirred on his arm, opened its mouth, and made a remark. Mr. Bumps had never paid much attention to foreign tongues, and he did

4

not understand what it said. Nevertheless, he knew what it *meant*. He knew for certain that the tiny, liquid syllables which had issued from the small mouth were a message from friend to friend.

He bade a cheerful good-by to the chief, kissed his hand to the black lady who had brought the monkey into his hut, and went off again down to the river. He took aboard *The Old Lion* a good store of nuts, bananas, and other fruit; and as that evening he looked back at the coast, shining in the last of the sun—and *The Old Lion* was now some miles out to sea—he turned to his monkey and said, "How do you like the sound of the name Jasper, sonny?"

The monkey softly turned to him as if to answer, but this time said nothing.

So Jasper he was called, although this was really due to a mistake on the part of Mr. Bumps. What had come into his mind, as he stood at the taffrail looking back at the coast of Africa, were the first two lines of a hymn that had been a favorite of his mother's—

> *From Greenland's icy mountains*
> *To India's coral strand.*

But in saying the words over to himself he had got the last but one word wrong. He had said:

From Greenland's icy mountains
To India's jasper *strand.*

Still, Jasper, he thought, was a better name than Coral, and Jasper it remained.

There never was a monkey so quick to learn, so grave in the learning, and so quiet and pleasant in manner as Jasper. Mr. Bumps could only guess how old he was, and he guessed, "p'raps five." And since the famous little son of John Evelyn even before this age could all but talk in Greek, Latin, and Hebrew, it may not be so marvelous as it sounds that Jasper soon began to pick up a few words of English. Long before this, however, he had learned to sit at table and say his grace (in his own tongue) ; to use a knife and fork, and a mug for his drink; to bow when spoken to; to swing his own hammock, and little things like that.

He would creep up, too, to watch the man at the wheel or the cook at his cooking in the galley or caboose. He would gaze for minutes at a time at the compass and lamp in the binnacle, and would salute the captain whenever he saw him on the bridge. He knew the Christian names of every man jack of the crew, and where each of them slept in the fo'c'sle; he could manage a little rope splicing, and knew the difference between a granny and a reef knot, a loop

and a fisherman's bend! In spite of his red cossack gown, he could scamper up the rigging to the truck or very summit of the mainmast twice as quick as any cabin boy, though no cabin boy of course has any tail to help.

Besides all this, Mr. Bumps taught Jasper much else. Not that he sat him down and *made* him learn. It amused him and Jasper enjoyed it. It was a long voyage, too. *The Old Lion* edged into the doldrums and there was plenty of time.

As the days and weeks drew by, Jasper became as much at home on *The Old Lion* with his friend Mr. Bumps as if he had been born to the sea. Merely because he was jimp and hairy, had a small, flat-nosed face, and showed his teeth when he talked, the sailors at first would tease and laugh at him, deeming him only a pet or a plaything. As soon as he began to talk King's English, however, they teased him no more. He said things they remembered.

What Mr. Bumps meant to do with him when he was safe home in his little house in Portsmouth he hardly knew. He was sure his wife, whose name was Emma, would be pleased to see his new friend, and there was no doubt at all about Topsy, Emmanuel,

8

and Kate. But how could he ever part with Jasper now? Yet how expect him to lead a sea life? There was, however, no need to decide anything for the present; and meanwhile he took almost as fond a care of him—sought him out dainties, physicked him when sick—as Mrs. Bumps was taking of their little Kate.

At last, and Mr. Bumps had long since made up his mind that he could never of his own wish be separated from Jasper, *The Old Lion* drew into the English Channel. She was nearly home. And one misty afternoon in November she sailed slowly up the Thames and dropped anchor in the Pool of London. It was bitter cold, but still, and a haze of the color of copper hung over the mighty city. And there in the midst, like an enormous leaden beehive against the sullen sky, rose the dome of St. Paul's.

Mr. Bumps stepped ashore early next morning, with the monkey hooded upon his arm, some presents for his wife and children in his bag, and set out briskly for his railway station. He had not been in old England for many months, and the first thing in his mind was to get down to Portsmouth as soon as he possibly could. But the haze that had been high over the city the day before had now descended into its streets, and

9

Mr. Bumps had to grope on in the direction of the Monument and Pudding Lane through a fog which grew steadily denser.

He knew, at last, that he had lost his bearings. And when presently he came to a little public house, *The Three Swans,* its windows dimly glowing in the fog, he decided to go in and ask his way. But, somehow or other, he didn't like the notion that Jasper should go in, too. He glanced into the little face under its hood, and saw how cold and doleful it looked. But he was afraid the thick tobacco smoke and the smell of the beer and spirits in *The Three Swans* might make him ill.

So, "Sit you here a moment, Jasper," he said, as he put him down beside his bag beside the lamppost, "and don't 'ee stir till I come back."

But, alas, Mr. Bumps stayed many minutes longer than he had intended to inside *The Three Swans,* and when he came back, though his bag was still there where he had left it, Jasper was gone.

Indeed, Jasper had been patiently waiting in the fog in the dim light of the lamppost for no more than five of them, when a stranger, with a black hat on his head, a black beard, and a coat reaching almost to his heels, had come by. If the monkey had not stirred at that

moment, all might have been well. But, at sound of these footsteps in the strange, cold London street, the solitary creature had lifted his face and put out a hand, for he had made many friends on board ship. And the stranger stooped and looked at him.

Now, by a chance, whether evil or not it is hard to say, this man with the dark beard was a dealer in all kinds of animals. He had a shop in a narrow alley not far from the river. That shop went back, and every now and then up two or three steps, at least forty paces. And from end to end of it there were cages of all kinds of birds and small beasts, besides tanks of fish and of rare snakes and lizards, and even gauze-covered cages of butterflies on rows of shelves. His larger animals he kept, though out of the rain, in a stone-flagged yard.

He stooped down, his rusty, black coat brushing the paving stones, and in the foggy gloom looked long into Jasper's face. Then he took the little, narrow hand in his, and gently shook it.

"How d'ye do?" he said, in a wheedling voice, and speaking through his nose. "Very pleased to meet you, I'm sure."

And Jasper, with his usual gentle manners, and thinking no harm of him, looked up into his face and

12

chattered a few sounds, which were uncommonly like sea-English.

The stranger shot one swift, thieflike glance over his shoulder, then, opening a button of his greatcoat, gingerly lifted Jasper from where he sat, slipped him in under it, and strode rapidly away.

Before evening, Jasper found himself, with a few monkey nuts and a can of water, squatting alone in a cage, surrounded by other cages in which, besides barking dogs and scrambling puppies, were scores of white rabbits and rats and cats—Manx, tabby, and Siamese—squirrels, ferrets, stoats, tortoises, owls, love-birds, canaries, parrots, parakeets, and macaws; and in the midst of a din and screaming of voices more deafening by far than he had ever heard in his own West African forests, or in the middle of a storm at sea. He sat shivering and trembling in his gown, and at last pushed his head in under its furry hood, muttering to himself in small, mournful, monkey accents, "Mr. Bumps. Mr. Bumps. O Mr. Bumps!"

But Mr. Bumps, having in great grief given up his friend for lost, was long since in the train and on his way in spite of the fog to his little square-windowed house in Portsmouth, and back to his Emma, his Topsy, Emmanuel, and Kate.

13

Jasper did not stay long in Mr. Moss's animal shop, only for nine days and nine nights. But at the end of them he had already begun to pine and droop, could scarcely eat, and seldom opened his eyes. He missed his friend the sailor, and his care and kindness; though whenever Mr. Moss himself, or the sharp-nosed, tallow-faced young man that helped in the shop, looked in at his cage and spoke to him, he looked solemnly back, without showing either his teeth or his temper. He never clutched at his food when it was pushed in through the wire door, nor did he even attempt to make any sound in response to what they said to him. He sat there, his hands folded under his gown, like some small, hairy king deprived of his kingdom. Mr. Moss and his young man had never seen his like before, and even in this short time they had both discovered that they could not face out the little creature's dwelling eyes.

But though Jasper sat for the most part so quiet and motionless in his cage that he might seem, at first sight, to be fast asleep, or even stuffed, all day long his ears and wits (and now and then his eyes) were busy. He would watch the Belgian canary birds which Mr. Moss, during their molting, had fed on special seed and cayenne pepper to brighten their feathers, for

14

hours at a time. There was an enormous python, too, coiled up in straw not far away, and for a long time he hardly dared to look at it. But at last he made himself watch that too; and he never ceased to listen to the talk between Mr. Moss and his tallow-faced assistant, and the strange human beings that came into the shop. Strange talk in the shop, too, he heard between his fellow captives.

Mr. Moss himself, though if Jasper had been like other ordinary monkeys he would have soon forgotten it, never felt *wholly* at ease at the thought that he had stolen this one. Odd, unlucky things began to happen in the shop. He himself upset a glass case full of death's-head moths. It frightened him—their tiny feet on his skin and the fanning of their sepulchral wings. The python one night, having managed to glide out of her tank, devoured a mandarin duck at one gulp, and escaped into London. And when his assistant, first thing in the morning, tripped over a broom that had been left on the floor of the shop and broke his left leg, his master began to think that it would be as well to get rid of Jasper as soon as he could.

So when one afternoon an acquaintance of his, who had once been a showman and trainer of animals for

16

a circus, stepped into his shop and inquired how much he wanted for Jasper, the price he asked him was so very moderate that his friend paid it down at once and carried the monkey off with him, there and then. At first sight of Jasper he, too, had become homesick for the ring lights and the tan and the tinsel and the ambling horses, and had determined to begin again.

"And what do you call him?" he asked Mr. Moss.

"Call him? Why, what he calls hisself, day in, day out, and even in his sleep!—Jasper."

"Ah, now, Jasper?" repeated his friend.

He was a dark man, hollow-cheeked and lean; and he wore his hair long over his ears. His name was Mr. J. Smith, but he changed this on the programs and playbills, when he was showing his animals, to Signor Dolcetto Antonio. Unlike one or two black-hearted miscreants who followed his trade, he believed in kindness and common sense.

"There are five things," he would say to his wife, "all things breathing—buffalos to bullfinches—*need;* like you and me, Amy: food, shelter, sleep, company, and freedom." And he gave his animals nearly as much as they could wish of them—all except the last.

Away from the cold and noise and stench and darkness of Mr. Moss's shop, Jasper soon began to be himself again. His appetite returned, his eyes brightened, he looked sleek and nimble. He was soon as well as could be expected, with his bosom friend Mr. Bumps gone, and himself so far from his own land.

In order to take all possible care of his charge, Signor Antonio brought him home to where he lived with his wife, in the upper parts of a house in Jay Street, Soho. Part of this house was a shop that sold wine and oil and coffee and macaroni and olives and sausages and other kinds of foreign meats and drinks. In the rest, first floor to roof, lived Mr. and Mrs. Smith. Here, beside the fire in their small parlor, they made Jasper as cosy as they could—in a little chamber to himself.

For two hours every morning, Signor Antonio would talk to Jasper and teach him tricks. When he was gone out to do his business, Mrs. Smith, busy herself over her cooking and housework, would talk to him, too. She was a very stout woman, much stouter than the chief of the Mlango-Nlangoes. And, like the chief, she was full of good humor and had a kind heart. She took particular pleasure in children and animals; and at the Zoo would not only cheep to the birds and stroke the gazelles, but nod and smile at the orangutans and hippopotami. She treated Jasper as if he were a long-lost son.

Her husband had soon discovered that Jasper was a monkey that had no equal. He was as different from other monkeys as chalk from cheese. He learned everything he was taught with ease and alacrity, and could soon chatter away to his friend, almost as if he had known English all his life. If he *looked* five, he could certainly *talk* like two and a half. But, though he was so teachable and sweet-tempered and serious in his manners, there was something about him that never ceased to perplex Mr. Smith.

He felt this in particular when, his lessons done, Jasper would sit quietly in his chair, waiting for his midday meal. He had an air, at such times, as if he were brooding on something of which Mr. Smith had not the least notion. He seemed to be so far away that even Mr. Smith never ventured to ask him what he was thinking about, or to summon him back to dark Soho.

Merely to look at, Jasper was a comfort to the eye. Mr. Smith, though he was a good-natured man, was as awkward and clumsy as a saucepan with too long a handle to it. He was all angles. Mrs. Smith, who was even more good-natured than her husband, sat and talked with no more grace than a feather bed. But Jasper, even in the least motion of his small body, turn of the head, of the hand, of the foot, was quiet as flowing water and delicate as the flowers beside it. When he touched, it was as if thistledown had settled at his finger tips. When he stretched out his fingers to take an apple, it was like the movement of a shadow through the air. He would sidle along Mrs. Smith's curtain rod without stirring one wooden ring; and if she were near, would be allowed to follow her out on to the roof where she sometimes sat, in spite of smoke and smuts, sewing a hem and looking over London. Jasper would balance himself in his gown on the edge of the tallest of the red chimney pots, glancing north, south, east, and west, and not a finger tip to keep his balance!

If he was this to look at, what can he have been in his secret mind—with its memories and dreams and sedate ponderings, river and forest, the terrors and dangers and delights of vast Africa, or rather of his own particular dark green corner of it?

W HAT I feel about our friend over there," Mr. Smith said to his wife one day, when Jasper sat asleep in his chair, "what I feel is, that he could learn me a sight more than I can learn *him*—of what, I mean, *matters,* my love. He's that privy yet polite you don't know where you are. And what I feel, *too,* is that there's something little short of shameful in letting a mere mob of humans come paying their half crowns and shillings and sixpences just to stare at him. He talks to us; but, bless you, he only talks to us about what he knows we can understand. He don't tell us his secrets. Never. The truth is, he ought not to have been took away from where he came from, though where *that* was, nobody knows. No Moss ever got such a mystery by rights. Never. He's had a queer past, has that little monk; mark *me*."

And Mrs. Smith, though in her heart she agreed with her husband, thought it would be unwise to say so.

"Don't you fret, Jim," she replied. "He has plenty to eat and keep him busy. Worry! Not he! Look at him there, sleeping as peaceful as a baby, as if there wasn't a coconut or a black man in the world. He's as happy as the day is long."

"Coconuts!" said her husband, but he was not convinced.

At last, one early morning, a happy thought came into Mrs. Smith's mind.

"What by and by would be really fair and square, Jim," she said, as she was combing her hair by the glass, "what by and by would be nice and proper, would be for you to take half of what you make out of Jasper, and him take the other half. Once he began to earn a bit of money, we could teach him what money *means*. After all, Jim, it's only a sort of short cut for bread and cheese and tables and chairs and clothes and houses—not to mention the time what's taken in making them; and he would soon pick it up. Then, maybe, he might like to get a few little things for himself.

23

He might like to set up, with some cash in the bank, as an independent gentleman. Judging from what *I've* seen of the world, he has twice as much sense as most such, and not a shadow of any vices; and I don't see *any*thing against it."

Mr. Smith looked at his wife in astonishment. Nor was it merely because she had been speaking with her mouth full of hairpins. It was because she would seem for days together not to agree with a single word he said, and then, of a sudden, out would come a notion that made everything plain and easy. So it was with Jasper.

About nine months after he had brought him home, Mr. Smith became perfectly certain that there was nothing else he could teach his charge. Jasper could make a speech, could sing, and draw pictures of forests and ships with a box of colored chalks. He could scribble down simple sums up to fractions on a blackboard, and find an answer. He could manage everything to the last nicety with his clothes. During the week he was dressed in scarlet breeches and a green coat, with ivory buttons. On Sundays, he wore a lightly starched ruff round his neck, a gown to his heels, and fine shoes. For out-of-doors he had two or three different cloaks. Not that Mr. Smith *kept* him to human clothes, or human ways either. Jasper agreed he must grow used to them. Whenever he so fancied, he went bare; and, if he wished, he kept two Sunday-clothes days in one week. But this was very seldom.

He knew many simple rimes, and Mr. Smith had made a little harp for him—very rough but tunable. To this he would sing these rimes, and other airs, and a curious music also, whose meaning he kept to himself. More than once, indeed, Mr. Smith had been awakened early in the morning to hear Jasper playing on his harp in the next room. And *then,* while both the words and tune seemed to be of his own making or remembering, there sounded a cadence in them that almost made him weep. By good fortune Mrs. Smith slept far heavier of nights than he did.

Anyhow, there was no doubt at all, that if Signor Antonio and Doctor Jasper—as they called themselves in the playbills—were ever to get rich, now was the time to begin. Mr. Smith had long since been to see the manager of the bank in which he kept his savings, and had arranged with him to open an account in Doctor Jasper's name. Into this each week he afterward paid Jasper's share of their takings, which mounted up by leaps and bounds.

"You see," he had first explained to the manager, "it may be some time before my young friend is able to come and pay his money in himself. But I want everything open and aboveboard. When he makes his debboo, which will be shortly, he will take half the fees and I shall take half. And when we have made what he thinks is enough, then he shall choose as he thinks best."

The manager, Mr. Johnson, who until then had seen only a few photographs of Doctor Jasper, not very good likenesses either, smiled at this arrangement. But there was no doubt that it *was* all open and above-board, and he fell in with Mr. Smith's wishes.

It was in the month of December that Doctor Jasper made his first appearance on the stage. This was in London. There was sleet that Christmas, and a cold wind was blowing in the lamplit London streets, when Signor Antonio and Mrs. Smith set off together in a four-wheeled cab bound for the *Fortune,* a famous theater which had been named after the old *Fortune* in the days of Queen Bess, and the Merry Wives of Windsor. "And not much more than twenty years after it was built," Mr. Smith told Jasper, "it was burned down to the very ground—in two hours."

"In two hours!" said Jasper.

Still, Mrs. Smith, as she reclined quietly but firmly against the purple velvet of the cab, her back to the horse and her face to Jasper, and her husband beside her to keep out the draft, might herself have been one of those merry wives come to life again!

In the clear cold north wind, the tiny snowflakes vanishing as they fell through the dark air, and with its multitudes of people going off about their pleasure in their furs and wraps and winter clothes, London looked as bright as a peep show.

Jasper trembled a little, and not from cold, as he gazed out of the glass cab window at the passers-by. Mr. and Mrs. Smith talked cheerfully to keep his spirits up, and sometimes made wonderfully good fun together about some overdressed lady or gentleman they could admire from their little inside gloom in the cab without themselves being seen. For *their* hearts, too, were beating high. But he, himself, in his warm dark corner, said nothing. The cab trundled along down the Charing Cross Road and into Trafalgar Square. Mr. Smith had told the cabman to take this way round to the theater because he wanted Jasper to see the lions.

"And look, Jasper," said Mrs. Smith, when her husband had pointed them out, "*that* there up there is the great Lord Nelson; and mighty cold he must be in his cocked hat—and only one eye and one arm, pore feller—with all that sleet falling up among them stars."

Jasper lifted his quiet face and could but faintly detect the great silent granite figure aloft against the sky.

"Sea," he muttered. "Seaman." But, strangely enough, Mrs. Smith, who was usually quickness itself at following what he said, supposed he meant to spell the word *see* and not *sea,* and was afraid he must be very nervous indeed of what lay in front of him if he had gone back to his old childish way of speaking— *See . . . Man . . .* when he had first learned English. But Jasper had other thoughts.

The cab rolled on along the Strand, and there was still enough melting sleet in the street almost to silence its iron-tired wheels. On and on it went, past the brightly lit shops and the hurrying people; and in a little while drew up in a back street where an iron lamp jutting out over the pavement lit up the stage door.

Mr. Smith then got out of the cab. He paid the fare, and (as much for his own good luck as for the cabman's) gave him a half crown over. And he asked him to be waiting for them at eleven. "Eleven sharp," he said.

Then, having handed out Mrs. Smith, he mounted the three steps, pushed open the door, which clapped-to after them with a bang that shook poor Jasper to the heart, and they all three entered the theater.

"Good evening, Sam," said Mr. Smith to the stout man sitting in a box behind a little open window by the door.

"Good evening," he replied, but his watery, gray eyes were fixed not on Mr. Smith but on Jasper. With a turn of his small head and a touch of his fingers, he had shown his friend that he wished to be put down. So, one after the other—Mr. Smith, Jasper, Mrs. Smith— the three of them ascended the flight of stone steps into the dressing room that had been set apart for them by the manager of the theater. And here Mr. Smith helped Jasper to spell out the description of himself that had been printed in large capital letters on the playbill, a copy of which was pinned to the wall. THE FIRST APPEARANCE OF THE LEARNED AND FAMOUS DOCTOR JASPER, he read out slowly, Jasper sagely nodding his head at every word, THAT MINUTE MARVEL OF MONKEYLAND, AND MASTER MIMIC OF MAN!

"There," said Mrs. Smith, "that's *you,* Jasper! What do you think of that?" But Jasper made no answer. At this moment, trembling a little, he was gazing at the picture of himself underneath the print. It had taken him straight home again—since the artist, though no doubt he had done his best, had made him look very much like a small gorilla!

When, with deft, fat hands Mrs. Smith had put the finishing touches to his toilet, and her husband was ready, they all three went down the stone steps again and made their way to the wings of the stage. There, in shadow and in silence, they waited. Soon it would be Jasper's turn. In this nook of the painted scenery— all flowers and trees and butterflies—the framework of which went up into the blaze of lights above, Jasper peered about him. It was the night after Christmas, and the theater, from the floor up to its very roof, was packed with human beings of all ages, but, particularly, children.

By standing on tiptoe and peeping through a tiny hole in the canvas, Jasper could see row above row of strange faces mounting higher and higher, their eyes fixed on the five *Exceptionally Elegant Ethiopian Elephants Engaged at Enormous Expense* which were now seated around their trainer on the stage. At sight of all these faces a sigh shook him from head to foot. And he turned away his head—and peered out to see the elephants themselves.

Four of these mighty animals, garlanded with mistletoe, were caparisoned in bright green and silver. The fifth, and the smallest, was dressed up as a clown, his face whitewashed, and one eye surrounded with a diamond in red. They sat on their tubs. They wreathed their proboscises. They greeted their trainer in a chorus that drowned even the blare of the band. They walked on their hind legs; they passed the bottle; they turned the handle of their hurdy-gurdies; and the two senior elephants danced a cumbrous polka, while the two juniors sat fanning themselves, and the youngest with a painted poker beat time.

Then, one by one, these sage and monstrous beasts, their tiny eyes alight with excitement, stumpy tails aswing, trailed off the stage to their own quarters. The curtain descended. It was Jasper's turn.

And soon all was made ready for him. A table, with books upon it, an empty inkstand, some foolscap, and a dinner bell; two gilt chairs covered in bright blue satin beside it, and a sofa—this was the only furniture, apart from an umbrella stand, a palm in a pot, and a red-and-green Axminster rug.

The music stopped. The curtain slowly rose again. And there, in the middle of the stage, was Signor Antonio, dressed up like a lackey in a black tail coat, and as if engaged in putting the room in order in preparation for the coming home of his master. And while he tidied the books and gave a last flick of his feather brush over the fleckless satin chairs and the palm in the pot, he kept talking to himself, though loud enough for everybody to hear. He was explaining who he was—the faithful servant of the great Dr. Themistocles Marmoset Jasper, the kindest and wisest master manservant ever had, and the most famous medico in Europe.—"In Europe, did I say?" he cried to himself, slapping his leg with his brush. "Nay, in the WORLD!"

"*Now,* Jasper," whispered Mrs. Smith, stooping over her small friend's head. "*World,* Jasper: that's your word, that's your cue! On you go, and bless you, Jasper! And if, poor mite," she breathed to herself, "you're half as nervous of the business as I am, in spite of my size, well . . . *Now,* Jasper!"

Jasper looked up at her; he let go her hand. Out of the shadows he went, and into the light.

34

In his striped trousers, French-gray waistcoat, long, black morning coat, with his gold watch chain and starched collar, high hat in hand, he minced gently forward. His patent-leather shoes were a little too long for him, but he managed them with ease.

At sight of his master, Jennings at once stepped forward. Doctor Jasper gave him his hat, his cane, and his canary-colored gloves. "Thank you, sir. Very good, sir," said Jennings. He hung the hat on a peg and stood the cane in the stand.

The Doctor lifted his head a little as he came to the low table, and reaching up, laid his hand upon a book. "It's a fine ssunny morning, Jennings," he said. "Who iss my firsst pay-sshent today?"

So dead a silence hung in the theater at first sound of these small treble words and their soft-hissed s's one could not only have heard a pin drop, but could have declared whether it had fallen on its head or its point! Then a little girl, in a seat high up in the dress circle, began to whimper a little. But she was soon hushed, and Jennings was explaining to his master that his first patient was the Right Honorable the Countess of Crumpet; "and a very nice lady too, sir, as I have been told; closely related to Lord Muffin, sir, of Teacake Castle."

Thereupon his master drew his watch from his pocket, and said: "It iss five minut'ss after ten, Jennings. I fear her lady-sshipp iss late."

"I will see, sir," said Jennings; "she may be in the anteroom." And he retired.

"It's all right, Ma; it's all right," he whispered to Mrs. Smith, as, swift and quiet as a shadow, he went whisking by. "Don't worry. He's *safe*."

Meanwhile, and while he was gone, Jasper having taken a chair at the gilded table, drew the long goose-quill pen from out of the dry inkpot, and bending his small head till his flat nose almost touched the paper, pretended to write on it.

"That will be three guine'ss," he sighed to himself, almost like a miser as he scrawled with the pen. "Three more guine'ss!" But though he said these words *as if* to himself, they were loud enough, like Mr. Smith's, for everybody in the theater to hear; and yet they were said so solemnly that nobody laughed.

At this moment Signor Antonio came on to the stage again, from behind the wings. But while he had been gone, he had dressed himself up in a bonnet, a flounced purple skirt and bustle, with a long train, and he carried a green striped parasol. He was now, of course,

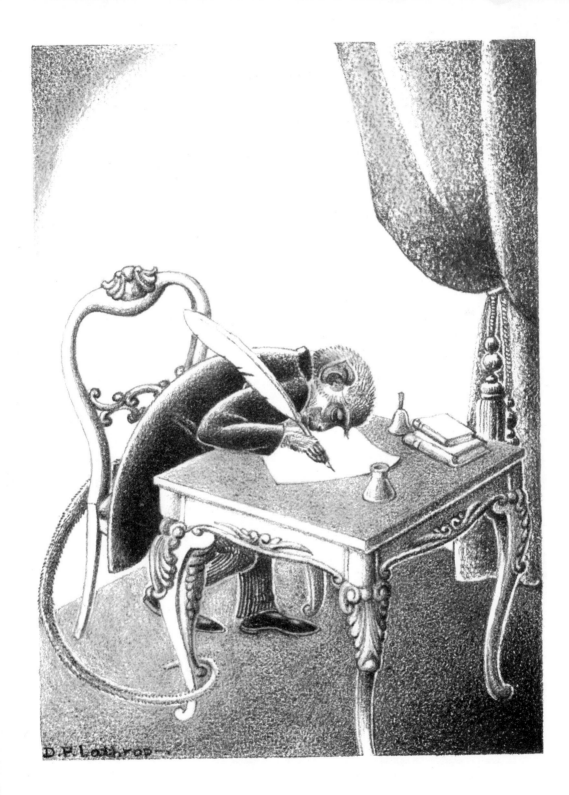

the Countess of Crumpet. Doctor Jasper bowed to the Countess, and they both sat down. And Doctor Jasper said to the Countess, "It iss a fine morning. Would your lady-sship, pleess, kindly put out the tongue?"

Then he stood up on his chair to look at her tongue, and said, "Ah! excussing me, your lady-sship, a ssorry tongue, a dreadful tongue." And still nobody laughed. But when the Countess, with a simper, thrust out a great man's hand in a white cotton glove from under her Paisley shawl for Doctor Jasper to feel her pulse— then *every*body laughed. And after that, except when Doctor Jasper was all alone on the stage, they hardly stopped to take breath.

And so the play went on, Jasper saying his part as if it were as simple and easy a thing to do as it is for other apes and monkeys to crack nuts and skin bananas. But though he seemed to all who watched from high and low in the theater to be as the manager had said he was—the Master Mimic of Man—this was not really true. This was only the human way of looking at him.

All the time he was really and truly himself, and only himself—thinking his own thoughts, gazing out of his bright, darting, round, dark-deepened, and now almost amber-colored eyes over the glare of the footlights at the people beyond, and at Signor Antonio in his shawl and gloves and bonnet and bustle. And though he smiled as he chattered, and even grinned with laughter when, owing to a mistake made on purpose, the Countess sat down on the floor instead of on her chair, he looked gravity itself underneath, if one could have seen him close.

It was cold to him in London—this wintry weather; and though he liked Mr. and Mrs. Smith, who had been very kind to him, and though he knew quite well in his own way of thinking what a pot of *money* meant, he had *not* liked the large, fat, black-mustached face of the manager of the theater, and had consented to shake hands with him only out of politeness. He took everything in good part. And yet, he pined still for a long-lost friend, and to return again to his own people.

And when the curtain fell at the end of his performance, his face shrunk up as if into a mask, and his eyes suddenly shut, at sound of the roar of voices that had broken out beyond it. Up went the curtain again —himself and Signor Antonio in the middle of the stage: and yet again and yet again—Doctor Jasper alone now; and again and again, now hand in hand with the manager on one side of him and Mr. Smith on

39

the other. It seemed as if the audience would shout themselves to a whisper and clap their hands off!

When at last the curtain came down and stayed down, he walked off a little dizzily and unsteadily, and clutched at Mrs. Smith's skirt. "Bless *me,* you poor, poor mite!" was all she could say to him, for there were tears in her eyes, part of rejoicing and part for pity, and she fondled his cold fingers as if he had been a child. But small though he was, even as monkeys of his kind go, he had been a gigantic success. The manager's face was one wide, dark, greasy smile when once more he shook hands with him, bowed to the ground, though it was not much more than in mockery, and said good-night.

So the money, Jasper's share, poured into the bank until he was by far the richest monkey in the world, even though he was, also, the only monkey in the world that knew it. Mr. and Mrs. Smith in all their dealings with him were as honest as the day, and they, of course, were soon rich, too.

NOW one day John Bumps came home again from sailing around the world, as he had sailed many times before, though never without pleasure. And even though he lived so far away from London as Portsmouth is, he had not been two days with his family before in large print in his newspaper he saw the name of Doctor Jasper, and read of what he had done.

"Jasper," he repeated to himself, "why that's queer, now, *that* is! Jasper!" He read it again and slapped his leg. "The same name, right enough," he said to himself. "And, Solomon Davy, surely there can't be two Jaspers, not like this! And if there are *not* two Jaspers, then this Jasper must be my Jasper!"

And there and then, he'd made up his mind, for he still had a good deal of money in his pocket after his voyage, that he would take Mrs. Bumps and Topsy and Emmanuel and Kate right up to London so that they could go to the *Fortune,* and see this Jasper with their own eyes. Even if he were not his old friend of the Mlango-Nlangoes and only a coincidence, it would be a Treat. And Mr. Bumps always gave his family a Treat when he came home from sea. He said nothing whatever to the children meanwhile about his friend Jasper in case it should prove a disappointment, though he told Mrs. Bumps. The following Saturday morning, having locked up the house, they all set out together in their best clothes, and caught an early train.

Emmanuel and Kate had never been to London before. They sat, each of them in a corner, staring out of the carriage window so intently at the fields and meadows and villages and churches and hills and farms gliding by that they both of them had only just finished the buns Mrs. Bumps had bought for them to eat on the journey when the train steamed into the great glass-roofed cavern of a station called Waterloo—after (as Mr. Bumps explained) the great Duke of Wellington, the Iron Duke, Old Nosy.

They had the whole day before them, and Mr. Bumps, when he gave them a Treat, never wasted a minute. He at once led them all off into an omnibus and they went, first to Westminster Abbey, then to see the soldiers on their horses in Whitehall, then to St. Paul's Cathedral. And there Mr. Bumps showed them through the brass grating where the body of Lord Nelson reposed in his tomb made of the cannon he had captured from the French. "He was a great sailor, was Lord Nelson," said Mr. Bumps.

"Do you mean a sailor just like you, Daddy?" piped out Topsy.

"Ssh! Topsy!" whispered Mrs. Bumps. "You mustn't call out like that. It's a church."

In St. Paul's Churchyard, on a seat in the open—for the sun was shining, though it was rather cold—they ate the lunch which Mrs. Bumps had packed into her wicker basket. Then, after seeing where the two little Princes had slept for the last time in the Tower of London, they had tea in a tea shop. The three children had a boiled egg each, but Mr. and Mrs. Bumps preferred theirs poached. After that they had some Bath buns and plenty of cake. Then they all went out again. And after letting them look for a little while into the shop windows in Cheapside, and especially a toyshop bowered in with a great plane tree like an

44

immense umbrella, Mr. Bumps—as if he had suddenly made up his mind—packed them all into a hackney cab and off they went to the *Fortune*.

Though Mr. Bumps was now first mate of *The Old Lion,* he was not yet a rich man, so he could not afford to take tickets for the seats downstairs, except in what is called the Pit. And he did not take tickets for the Pit because Mrs. Bumps said she always liked to look down when she went to a theater. They were extremely early and by good luck there were five seats available in the Upper Circle, and these in the very middle of the front row. Very pleased they were to be able to sit quietly in these stuffed easy seats and to rest and watch the people, after walking about such a long time in London. Indeed, they had hardly settled themselves in, when little Kate, who was only five and tired out, fell fast asleep in her chair.

Topsy and Emmanuel, however, stayed wide awake, sucking their peardrops (because Mrs. Bumps had thought the seats too dear for bull's-eyes) , and whispering and chattering and watching everything that went on. They had never in all their lives seen so many fine ladies with bare shoulders and diamonds in their hair, or so many gentlemen in long, black coats and tall collars.

45

One by one the members of the band, some carrying their instruments, came edging their way to their seats in front of the stage, and began to tune up or softly tootle on their oboes and trombones. The drummer, too, thumped softly on his drums, but not on his triangle or cymbals. And last came the conductor with his ivory wand.

"What's that for?" chirped Emmanuel.

"That," said Mrs. Bumps, "is to do the music with."

The conductor sat down on his little velvet seat and waited.

Mr. Bumps took out his silver watch. "Sharp on the hour," he whispered to Mrs. Bumps. "I wonder what they are waiting for."

He had no need to wonder long. For suddenly at a signal the conductor with white-gloved hand lifted his wand, and to a crash of music that nearly startled poor little Kate out of her wits, everybody in the theater stood up and the band played the National Anthem. Sure enough, in a moment or two there came into a great box beside the stage which had been trimmed up with holly and mistletoe, first the King of England himself, then the Queen, then their son, the Prince of Wales, and then a little foreign princess with black

46

ringlets and a tiny fan. They were followed by a few nice-looking but splendid ladies and gentlemen; and the King stood in front of the box, in the middle of it, while the anthem went on.

"That's the King," whispered Mr. Bumps to Emmanuel.

"And that's the Queen," said Mrs. Bumps. "And there, see, Topsy, see, Manny, see, Kitty, that's the Prince of Wales!"

It was a long time before little Kate could see at all, she had been so dead asleep. When the last note had been played, they all five cheered as loud as they could, and so did the other people in the theater. The King bowed. They cheered again. Then he sat down; and slowly, quietly, in heavy folds, the curtain ascended and the performance began.

First came acrobats, in tights and spangles. Next came a juggler and his small daughter. It looked as if the balls and hoops and dinner plates they juggled with were things alive. After the juggling there came a man who sang "The Bay of Biscay," though Mr. Bumps knew a good deal more about the Bay than he did. And after him the five silent-footed Ethiopian Elephants debouched one after the other on to the stage.

47

At the sight of them, though the three children opened their mouths like O's and clapped till it hurt, Mr. Bumps himself could scarcely breathe. But not of course because he had never seen elephants before. Far from that. He had seen quantities of elephants—either walking about, wild and tranquil, in the black man's swamps in Africa, or lying caked with mud in the heat of the tropic sun, or fountaining one another with cascades of silvery water at the close of day. And even though these five did clever tricks, he had watched others at far more useful ones in their own country. Not that he despised the elephants, he was only used to them.

No; Mr. Bumps was waiting for Doctor Jasper and could scarcely endure the delay. He was waiting for Doctor Jasper in his "Grand New Act"—as the play-bills said, an act "especially invented for the August Amusement of Royalty; and patronized by the Shah of Persia, the Emperor of Abyssinia, and other all-powerful Potentates." And he knew now that before he could count fifty it would begin.

The huge, ponderous beasts, having bowed, kneeling, in their green and silver, to express their thanks for the applause, were shuffling off toward the back of the stage. There, as the lights dimmed, they stood in a row,

48

their trunks uplifted above their heads. There came a pause; and then a slender shaft of pearly light struck down from on high toward the wings. A sudden trumpeting broke out from the elephants' throats, a trumpeting loud enough to drown the strains of twenty orchestras.

And into the beam of light—it moving with him as he went—there came tripping softly forward—a trailing cloak of crimson velvet edged with real gold lace upon his shoulders, a tall cap of sable surmounted by a plume of *aracatan* feathers pinned with a diamond in front of it upon his head, a little silver-gilt scepter in his right hand—Jasper. No longer now a medico of fashion, prescribing pills for the Countess of Crumpet, but himself *Almighty Emperor of All the Ethiopians,* the All-Excellent Ammanabi Nana Dâh.

Following in his train came two small fuzz-wigged pygmy blackamoors in ostrich feathers and in robes of silk, of yellow and vermilion. One of these was carrying the Emperor's royal sunshade, and the other (for it was very light in weight) his gilded throne. And these were followed by Signor Antonio (Mr. Smith), no longer either a manservant or a countess, but one of the Emperor's tallest and lankiest wives!

When the trumpeting of the elephants had died

49

down and the cymbals and drums had ceased to sound, there went up such a roar of voices in the theater from the people in it that it was heard outside for half a mile in all directions. Even the King of England, seated smiling in his Royal Box, could not remember to have been greeted with a louder *Huzza*. And then, almost as if this prodigious noise itself had caused it, an utter quiet fell. The Emperor, having gathered his crimson skirts around him, his scarlet sunshade like a huge mushroom over his head, had taken his seat upon his throne. The royal twelve-whiskered leopard skins had been laid about his feet.

He sat there a moment—small, upright—perfectly still, and looked on them all. Not a tongue wagged, not a sigh or a cough sounded in all the theater. The *only* stir, and no one noticed it, was that little Kate, who had never before seen such things or anything like them, ducked down her head out of sight of the stage and hid her face in her mother's lap.

The Emperor Jasper looked around him. He was accustomed now to the glare and the sea of faces and the plaudits and the laughter. He knew where he was, and he knew too—though he himself alone could tell it—*who* and *what* he was. And perhaps for this reason,

50

as he sat there peering out of his splendor, the host of those who were looking at him felt a peculiar coldness stealing in their blood.

It was not only as if they were uneasy in his presence—the tiny, motionless head, the intent eyes—but also as if they were frightened. Even the Queen, in her disquiet, glanced sidelong at the King, but the King was looking at the Emperor. And the Emperor at this moment, having very gently lifted his minute left hand, had opened his lips to speak. . . .

Perhaps if Mr. Bumps had thought all this over for a moment or two he would have remained quietly seated with his family in the front row of the Upper Circle and would have said nothing. He would have waited till the end of the performance, and then found his way round to the Stage Door, and sent in to the Manager his card—his visiting card—which he had had printed when he had been made first mate of *The Old Lion: Mr. John Bumps, First Mate* of THE OLD LION, 7 *The Transoms, Portsmouth.* That would have been the right thing to do. But Mr. Bumps, being a seaman and not used to holding himself back when anything that needed doing was to be done, couldn't wait to think.

Out loud, the only sound in the theater, except that the Emperor having opened his lips had said, "We," he called "Jasper! . . ." And as if on one hinge every face in the theater, and every face even in the Royal Box, had turned round to look at him. Moreover the puny Emperor on the stage in his gold and crimson finery had said not a syllable after that first clear "We"—which he had pronounced as if it were spelled Oo-*ee*—but had looked at him, too. All else then but rapture had vanished out of his mind. And, in the twinkling of an eye, without the least haste, or word, or sound, or nod, he had risen from his throne, and was softly pattering toward the footlights, or rather to the side of the footlights opposite the Royal Box.

Now the stage was framed in, top and side, with a shimmering arch of carved wood and painted plaster. All kinds of knobbly fruits and flowers and little cupids and ribbons and dolphins and birds adorned it, glistening bright with gilt and colors. It was behind this arch that the curtain rolled down, and the *Fortune* was one of the handsomest theaters in London.

In all that quiet, then, slowly and without haste, Jasper began to climb this arch, his royal robes swinging free behind him. They were heavy with their gold

53

lace, and he climbed slowly. But he climbed none the less surely, on and on, and up and up, and watched by every eye, until he had reached to where Mr. Bumps's gallery began. Here there ran a low wooden wall to keep the people from falling out of the gallery. Those in the front row of this gallery sat in their seats with their knees bent, looking over this low wall at the stage, and—to make it comfortable for their elbows as well as to look nice—the top of it had been padded with horsehair and covered with a maroon-colored stuff called plush.

So it was with no sound at all from his small five-toed feet that Jasper came—hastening, now—alone, along this wall in front of the people seated there, their faces in the reflected glow of the footlights looking as white as china. Straight along this dizzy path he silently tippeted until he reached the place where Mr. Bumps was sitting. There he stopped. He looked at Mr. Bumps and bowed his head. Then he said something that few heard and nobody understood. He put out his hands toward Mr. Bumps. And the two friends were restored to one another.

NOW all this time the people had sat perfectly still, watching. But when they witnessed what had happened—and these two there, Jasper and Mr. Bumps—though they didn't really know what to say or think, they all began to talk, and some to shout or even to hoot. They were angry. They were being cheated. *This* was not what they had paid all that money to see! Poor Mrs. Bumps could even hear what those near by were saying. She was growing more and more hot and discomfited. "O John! O John!" she kept repeating.

And now the manager, whom Jasper had come to like even less and less as his nights had gone by, appeared, marching on to the stage. He bowed to the

King, he bowed to the Queen, he bowed to the Prince of Wales, and he called out in a loud voice that he was very sorry for what had happened. He said he was very sorry to them all. He said that he had paid pounds and pounds of money for Jasper to come and amuse them, and now here was this man up there enticing him away. He bawled out, "Emperor Jasper, Emperor Jasper, come down, sir!"

Then some voices in the back parts of the theater shouted, "Turn him out!" and a great clamor began, some yelling this and some that, and the manager standing alone, fat and black and helpless in the middle of the stage, cajoling in vain Jasper to come back. As for Mr. Smith, since he was dressed up as one of the Emperor's wives, and was a born actor, he felt that it was not his place to speak, especially before royalty. His eyes rolled in his black-dyed face but he said nothing.

Meanwhile, safe with his Mr. Bumps again, Jasper had made not the faintest sign that he had ever heard the manager's call. And now, louder and louder, many voices were shouting, "Send him back!" and some were bellowing, "Let him stay!" And the uproar grew worse and worse.

D.P.Lathrop.

At last the King himself stood up in the Royal Box and raised his hand. There was at once a great hush in the theater. Everybody fell silent. The King said, "Whose monkey is this marvel?"

With a frowning countenance he looked down upon the manager. And the manager answered not a word. Then the King turned his eyes toward Mr. Bumps. He said, "Let that man stand up." And Mr. Bumps stood up.

"Who are you?" said the King.

"I am John Bumps, may it please your Majesty," said Mr. Bumps simply. "First mate of *The Old Lion,* now lying at Portsmouth."

"What are you doing here?" said the King.

"I came, your Majesty—and this is Mrs. Bumps beside me with the children—I came in hopes of seeing an old friend again."

"Who?" said the King.

Mrs. Bumps was now clutching tight her husband's hand, since it was hidden by the plush-topped wooden wall. His voice faltered. He touched with his other hand Jasper's sable cap.

"This, sir," he said.

"You mean," said the King, smiling, "his Serene

58

Mightiness, the All-Excellent Ammanabi Nana Dâh? Beseech his Mightiness to stand forth."

This good humor of the King greatly pleased all the people present, and every eye was now fixed on Mr. Bumps.

"*Now,* Jasper," whispered he, "the King of England is speaking to 'ee."

Jasper blinked but once at his old friend, pressed the finger clasped tight in his hand, and stood up on the plush parapet, before them all.

And the King, his eyes twinkling, said, "Is it your wish, cousin, that you remain with our loyal subject, Mr. Bumps, or"—and he swept his hand toward the manager and the footlights. An instant's silence followed.

And then, "Thissee Misster Bumpss, ssir," piped Jasper, for he had never quite mastered his s's, "thissee Misster Bumpss, ssir, iss my *firsst* friend. Mr. Ssmith iss my o-ther friend. My *firsst iss. . . .*" But the next word which was *firsst* was almost drowned by the shout of delight from a thousand throats that went up to the roof of the theater like the roar of an avalanche. It was fortunate for the manager that he had already left the stage and gone into the back parts of the theater.

59

And then and there Mr. Bumps and Mrs. Bumps and the three children and Jasper were conducted down to the Royal Box and were presented to His Majesty. And first the King and then the Queen and then the Prince of Wales and then the little foreign princess shook hands with Jasper, and he spoke to them. And the King slipped a ring off his own finger and hung it round the neck of the Ethiopian Emperor. They met, one might say, as equals.

But Mr. Bumps being a sailor and an honest man, when the theater was empty and the lights were out and the people gone away, sat down in a little back room behind the stage with the manager and Mr. and Mrs. Smith, while Mrs. Bumps and the children waited for them in Jasper's dressing room. Here, the four of them, over a bottle of port wine, made a bargain together, so that the manager should not lose too much money. The bargain was that for the whole of the next three days, except when it was time for dinner or tea, Jasper should sit on the stage of the *Fortune* in his gold and crimson, the King's ring dangling round his neck, his cap of sable on his head, while every man, woman, or child who wished and could pay to see him, passed along—in at one door and out at another—before his throne. And of the cash they might take at the doors, it was agreed that the manager should keep half, Mr. Smith a quarter, and Jasper a quarter. Mr. Bumps would take nothing. In those three days the manager made more profit than he had ever made before in a whole month!

When the three days were over, Mr. Bumps's leave from his ship was over, too, and they all went down to Portsmouth. By the kindness of the captain of *The Old Lion,* it had been arranged that Jasper should come aboard—it was his wish—and return to Africa. He might, if he had so chosen, have stayed in England and lived in a palace for the rest of his life. His fame had run like wildfire through the Kingdom, and far beyond it. Telegrams had come from Paris and Rome and Vienna and Budapest, and all parts of America, entreating him to visit them.

Apart from telegrams, the postman brought Jasper a small sack of letters every morning—from old ladies in the country who wished to adopt him, from learned professors of Oxford and Cambridge who wished to share his wisdom, from cunning men who hoped to make money out of him, and from all kinds of people grown-up and otherwise who asked him to put his name in their birthday books. And the King did not forget him. But Jasper refused everything—except the birthday books; he pined only for home.

In the meantime he himself made many presents to all his friends, and especially to little Kate, according to what he thought they would like best. The rest of his money—after he had said good-by to Mr. Johnson—had been packed in the cellar at the bank into twenty-eight small chests or coffers. These were piled up in the cabin that had been prepared for him on *The Old Lion*. And a nice pile they made.

Besides this, with the captain's consent, Jasper and Mr. and Mrs. Bumps had bought a large quantity of all kinds of trinkets, toys, linen and silk, dainties and beverages that would not rust or tarnish or go bad upon the voyage, whatever weather they might encounter. Jasper had thought of everything that his own people round about Dondo might fancy and enjoy. And the King had commanded that on this voyage *The Old Lion* should fly not the red ensign but at the main truck the Royal Standard.

A crowd of people so vast thronged the quay and the windows and the roofs of the houses near by to see Jasper off that some of those in the front row were

tumbled into the water. All except one had nothing worse than a sousing and were picked up by rowboats. But the manager unfortunately, who had pushed past some small boys for a better view, was drowned.

The best brass band in Portsmouth played *Rule Britannia,* and to the strains of *Rio Grande* the men of *The Old Lion* weighed anchor.

Oh *say,* were you ever in Rio Grande?—
　Awa-ay, Rio!
It's there that the rivers run down golden sand--
　And we're bound for the Rio Grande.
And awa-ay, Rio!—away, Rio!
Sing, fare you well, my bonny young gal,
　We're bound for the Rio Grande!

She shook, she stirred. Softly a gentle breeze between the blue sky and the sparkling water bellied out the sails of the ship. She drew away upon the water, past Nomansland Fort, where a gun puffed out to greet her, and smalled more and more. By the time Mrs. Bumps and the three children sat down to tea, she was out of sight of land.

Mr. Bumps had many a quiet and private talk with Jasper in his cabin as the days went by. Never had the old ship seen fairer weather. The two friends were

64

sad at heart, for Mr. Bumps knew that nothing he could say now would dissuade Jasper from returning to his own people. That, Jasper assured him, as well as what words he had could do so, was his *one* wish; and Mr. Bumps could say no more.

Now the head village where Mr. Bumps's friend, the chief of the Mlango-Nlangoes lived, was a mile or more from the banks of the Quanza. It lay beyond a swamp where there is a forest of mangroves, the abode of countless crocodiles, though the two-horned rhinoceroses keep to the river. Between the river and the swamp (where, if there were hundreds of crocodiles, there must have been thousands of monkeys!) was a stretch of sand and green.

In this spot, out of sight of the river, but well in reach of the trees, the black men whom Mr. Bumps's friend, the chief of the Mlango-Nlango tribe, had very kindly lent him for the purpose, brought up not only Jasper's crates and tubs and boxes and barrels of rare nuts and fruits, fruits in sirup, biscuits, beads, gewgaws, and so forth, but also his money chests crammed tight with sovereigns and silver. For nothing that Mr. Bumps or Mr. Johnson or Mr. and Mrs. Smith could say could persuade Jasper that all this money of his was just that and nothing more, and would be of no more use to his friends in their treetops, except perhaps for the beauty of it, than nutshells or pebble-stones. It had been given to him, he kept saying, for what he had done; and therefore he would like to take it all back to his people—except of course what he wished to spend on the presents he had given to Mr. Bumps and his other friends.

Since, then, Jasper, however much they argued, still wished to take back his money with him, Mr. Bumps had said of course, "Let it be so." Just as the King had said.

When all Jasper's possessions had been piled up in the open space between the hidden river and the forest which he had chosen for his camping place, and when a small bell tent had been pitched for him beside them, it was evening. Strange voices of all manner of animals and birds sounded in their ears when Mr. Bumps bade his friend good-night.

"I hope, Jasper," he said, "ay, and more than hope, that your kith and kin over there will be pleased to see you. I hope so. But they have been keeping mighty quiet." He said it with a faint heart, smiling at his little friend dressed up, as he had himself decided,

in his robes of gold and crimson, his sable cap on his head. Still, since Mr. Bumps had promised to come back in the morning, this was not good-by. It was only good-night.

When Mr. Bumps did come back in the morning, Jasper greeted him sadly enough. Though he had heard in the night faint chatterings and shufflings, not a single friend of all he had known in past times—not one—had come near him. So at Mr. Bumps's advice they unpacked some of the boxes and crates containing the dainties that smelled sweetest and strongest, and strewed them about in enticing piles some little distance away from Jasper's tent and nearer the forest.

Next morning these had vanished; and yet Jasper had remained solitary and unvisited in his tent all the night long. He had not slept a wink. Never mind, he told Mr. Bumps; his friends were no doubt shy and timid. He was sure they would be pleased to see him and longed to speak to him and welcome him back.

But morning after morning the piles grew less and less; the food was all gone; the toys and trinkets were scattered out of the boxes; only the money, the sovereigns and the silver, were left. And these the monkeys, having smelled and fingered them, left disowned.

Jasper thought at last it must be his royal robes,

68

his antelope slippers, his cap, and his colors that kept his people from knowing who he was. He said this, smiling, to his friend Mr. Bumps, but not as if he quite believed it.

That evening when they parted again, the air over Africa was heavy and stagnant and the sky lowering. Silent lightnings gleamed ever and again above the distant forests, and they could hear the tom-toms of the Mlango-Nlangoes sullenly drumming from their hidden dancing places. Jasper had stripped himself of all his finery, and stood up beside his tent only in his own fur—a little monkey, as he was before. Mr. Bumps shook him by the hand.

"Good-night, old friend," he said, "and God-speed."

When he came back the next morning after the storm, the cap and the robes and the slippers and the gilded scepter were gone. The tent had been blown away. And Jasper was gone, too. Mr. Bumps called and called and called. He came back in the evening and called again. No voice answered him. The forest lay dark and silent. Three days, by the kindness of the captain, to whom he had sent a black man as messenger, he waited and waited. But he waited in vain. And on the fourth *The Old Lion* sailed away.

—Used by permission of the publishers, Faber and Faber.

69